Quest for
the Queen

A Magical World Awaits You
Read

THE SECRETS OF DROON

#1 The Hidden Stairs and the Magic Carpet

#2 Journey to the Volcano Palace

#3 The Mysterious Island

#4 City in the Clouds

#5 The Great Ice Battle

#6 The Sleeping Giant of Goll

#7 Into the Land of the Lost

#8 The Golden Wasp

#9 The Tower of the Elf King

#10 Quest for the Queen

and coming soon

#11 The Hawk Bandits of Tarkoom

Quest for the Queen

by Tony Abbott
Illustrated by David Merrell

A
LITTLE APPLE
PAPERBACK

SCHOLASTIC INC.
New York Toronto London Auckland Sydney
Mexico City New Delhi Hong Kong

To Benjamin McCormack,
a good friend, faithful reader,
and wizard in the making

Book design by Dawn Adelman

ISBN 0-439-20784-3

Text copyright © 2000 by Robert T. Abbott
Illustrations copyright © 2000 by Scholastic Inc.
All rights reserved. Published by Scholastic Inc.

SCHOLASTIC, APPLE PAPERBACKS, and associated logos
are trademarks and/or registered trademarks of Scholastic Inc.

12 11 10 9 8 7 6 5 4   1 2 3 4 5/0

Printed in the U.S.A.   40
First Scholastic printing, November 2000

Contents

1. A New Kind of Homework — 1

2. Strange Strangers — 13

3. The Wonder in the Trees — 25

4. Into the Arena — 37

5. A Princess in Trouble! — 49

6. Droon's Funniest Man? — 57

7. Tarok's Mystery Wagon — 65

8. The Quest Begins! — 74

9. Island of Magic — 86

10. A Spell from the Past — 93

One

A New Kind of Homework

Rub! Scrub! Splash!

Eric Hinkle bent over the sink in the bathroom at school. He swished his hands in the soapy water, trying to clean up after gym.

"You're lousy at climbing ropes," he said to his friend Neal. "Did you have to fall on me?"

"I'm better at watching things than doing them," Neal said as he scrubbed dirt from his shirt, his nose, and his shoes. "I think it's a sign of smartness."

"That's not what the coach said," said Eric. Then he sighed. "Man, we need to go back."

"To class?" said Neal. "Mrs. Michaels promised us a math quiz. Can't we be a little late?"

Eric turned to face him. "No, I mean to Droon! I can't think about anything else."

It was true. Droon was always on Eric's mind.

It had all begun one day when he and Neal and their friend Julie were cleaning up his basement. Well, they were *supposed* to be cleaning up. Mostly they were playing around.

Then, behind some boxes, they had discovered a small closet. Inside the closet was a rainbow-colored staircase. It led to another world.

A magical world called Droon.

Neal splashed water on his nose. "I know what you mean. It's kind of boring here. Julie wants to go back, too. I just hope Keeah is okay."

Keeah was one of the first people the kids had met in Droon. She was a young princess learning to be a junior wizard. An old and very powerful wizard named Galen Longbeard was teaching her all the magic she needed to know.

But what Keeah wanted to know most was when her mother would be free of an evil spell.

For years, Keeah's mother, Queen Relna, had been changing into one animal after another. She had to go through many shapes until she could be human again.

At the end of their last adventure, Keeah had learned that the queen was now in the form of a red tiger.

To find her, Keeah had flown away on the back of a giant bird. The kids didn't know what had happened next.

"I wish we could go back whenever we want," said Eric. "I don't like waiting."

Usually, the kids dreamed about Droon. Sometimes Keeah sent them a message through an enchanted soccer ball. But until one of those things happened, Eric and his friends just had to wait.

Tap! Tap! There was a knock at the lavatory door. "Guys?"

It was Julie's voice. "Mrs. Michaels wants you back right now," she said. "It's quiz time."

Neal looked at his shirt in the mirror. It was soaking wet. "Well, my work here is done. See you in class." He left Eric alone at the sink.

Eric was about to drain the water when he glanced down. The soapsuds swirling in the sink suddenly stopped . . . in the shape of a face.

A sad old face. With a long white beard.

"Galen?" Eric mumbled to himself. "Galen!"

A moment later, the face in the sink was gone.

The water was just water.

Eric dashed back to class and slid into his seat between Julie and Neal. "I just saw Galen floating in the bathroom sink!" he whispered.

"How did he fit in there?" Julie asked.

"No! I mean, his face was in the soap!"

"Eric," said Mrs. Michaels, giving him a stern look. "We'll start our math quiz now." She passed out the papers and stood in front of the room. "You will have ten minutes to finish. Starting . . . now."

Eric looked at the paper but all he could think about was the wizard's face.

Why had Galen appeared to him? Why had he looked so sad? Was something wrong?

Eric felt a tug on his sleeve. It was Julie. She was staring at the chalkboard.

He looked up. He nearly fell out of his seat.

A piece of yellow chalk was floating up behind the teacher's back. Silently, it pressed against the green board and began to write.

Eric glanced around. Everyone else was busy working on the quiz. Their heads were down.

The chalk began to spell out letters.

S . . . h . . . e . . .

Eric slid his foot out and tapped Neal's sneaker. Neal looked up. His mouth dropped open.

. . . i . . . s . . .

The chalk hesitated as Mrs. Michaels

glanced at the clock. "Five more minutes," she said.

The chalk continued writing.

. . . l . . . o . . . s . . . t . . .

She is lost. Eric's eyes widened. *She? Keeah!*

Mrs. Michaels started to turn around.

Then the eraser flashed up from the bottom of the board and — *swish!* — wiped away what the chalk had written. Eric and his friends were the only ones to see the message.

They were the only ones *meant* to see it.

They were so excited they could hardly finish the quiz. When the final bell rang, they burst from the classroom and rushed out to their bus.

"Galen must have sent the message!" Eric whispered. "I think it's about Keeah."

Julie nodded. "She must have gotten

lost trying to find her mother. And now we need to find her!"

"It's like homework," said Neal. "Only from Droon!"

Ten minutes later, the bus stopped at their corner. They raced into Eric's house and were down in his basement in no time.

Neal and Julie pulled aside some heavy boxes. Behind the boxes was the door to a small closet nestled under the basement steps.

The kids piled into the closet and shut the door behind them. Eric looked at Julie and Neal.

"Everybody ready?" he asked.

They nodded.

Julie turned off the light. *Click.*

For an instant, the small room was dark. Then — *whoosh!* — the floor vanished beneath them, and they stood at the top of a long, shimmering staircase.

They never knew where the stairs would lead, only that one of their Droon friends would meet them at the bottom.

A warm wind blew as the three friends began to descend the stairs.

The sky around them was glowing pink.

"There's a coastline below," said Julie. "Some sand. Lots of sharp rocks. There's a big sea on one side and a forest on the other. It looks okay."

"I don't see anybody down there," said Neal. "Where's our welcome committee?"

"Let's just be careful," said Eric cautiously. "We can't be sure of anything."

That was true. There were lots of friendly creatures and people in Droon, but there were other types, too.

An evil sorcerer named Lord Sparr had long been trying to take over Droon. He was in hiding now, but the kids knew he could pop up at any moment.

As Eric looked out across the crashing waves, he also remembered the mysterious witch named Demither, who ruled under the sea.

The last time they saw her, Demither had transformed herself into a giant sea serpent.

Ka-splursh! Waves splashed over the rocks below.

"I see a boat!" said Julie, pointing to a small shape bobbing on the waters. "I bet it's Galen coming to welcome us."

"Yes, a friendly face," said Neal. "Let's hurry down and meet him."

They dropped onto the beach just as the staircase faded. They knew it would appear again when it was time to go home.

The boat headed toward them.

"He's trying to land," said Neal.

Ka-whoom! The sea thundered loudly, and a large wave rose up like a hand.

It seemed to grab the tiny boat and hurl it right at the shore.

Right at the jagged rocks.

"Oh, no! Galen's going to hit the rocks! He's going to crash!"

Two

Strange Strangers

Splurshhhh . . .

But the little boat didn't hit the rocks.

It slid neatly between them and up onto the sand. Then it stopped.

"Whoa," said Julie. "That was lucky."

"Or magical," said Eric with a smile. "Good thing for Galen that he knows so many spells."

The three friends ran over to the boat.

It was a small wooden craft with a short mast.

"Hello!" Neal called out. "Anybody at home? I mean . . . at boat!"

The boat jerked once, then — *flonk! whiz! blap!* — its wooden sides flapped down, a set of four wheels popped out from beneath it, the mast collapsed, and a seat flipped over on the front. In seconds, the boat was no longer a boat.

"It looks like a circus wagon," said Neal. "I love circuses!"

"Do you really think it's Galen's?" Julie asked.

Plonk! One last panel slid down into place.

"Not unless he changed his name," said Eric.

The wagon now bore a brightly painted sign:

Tarok the Clown!
Featuring Slag, Mightiest
Man in Droon!

"I love clowns!" said Neal.

Moments later, a door opened on the front of the wagon. Out popped a little man in a big coat. He had a funny horn stuck in his belt, his hair was blue, and his nose was big, red, and false.

He was mumbling quietly to himself but stopped when he saw the children.

Julie stepped forward. "Um . . . hello," she said. "We're glad you didn't crash —"

Honka-honka! The man squeezed his horn suddenly.

"I am Tarok the clown!" he blurted out. "I make millions laugh with my jokes. Here's one! What's the difference between children and fish? Give up? I *like* fish! Ha-ha!"

Eric and his friends looked at one another.

"Does he mean he doesn't like *us*?" Neal whispered.

Tarok jumped up on his seat and waved his arms. "Behold Slag, the Mightiest Man in Droon! Slag? Where are you? SLAG!"

Blam! The back of the wagon flew open and out stepped a large man. A very large man.

Slag was at least seven feet tall.

He had a head as large as a pumpkin and he seemed to be made entirely of muscles.

Julie nudged Eric. "He's bigger than the wagon!" she whispered. "How in the world did he fit in there?"

Slag grinned as he flexed his muscles. His smile showed many teeth missing.

"We're going to the Droon Quest!" said Slag. "In Bangledorn Forest!" He pointed at the wall of trees nearby. "That's the forest."

"Thanks," said Eric. "That's good to know. But what's a Droon Quest?"

Tarok narrowed his beady eyes at them. "The Quest is a great race for a wonderful prize. Everyone's coming from miles around to compete. And I'll be there, making them laugh. My partner, Slag, will perform feats of amazing strength. But right now, we're late. Slag, let's go!"

The giant then reached into the back of the wagon and pulled out a large colorful net made of thick rope. He tossed it over his shoulder.

Then he tugged on something else.

Hrrr! A large shaggy six-legged beast called a pilka clopped out of the wagon.

"Whoa!" said Julie, edging around to the back of the wagon. "What else is in there?"

Blam! Slag slammed the door before she could see inside. Then he hitched the pilka to the wagon, clambered into the seat next to Tarok, and set the net beside him.

"Can I ask what the net is for?" asked Neal.

"We're going fishing, of course!" said Tarok.

Julie blinked. "But you're heading to the forest. How can you fish in a forest?"

"That's the joke!" Tarok said without smiling. "See how funny I am?"

He squeezed his horn once more — *honka-honka!* — then snapped the reins. The yellow wagon sped quickly across the beach.

Eric waited for it to disappear into the forest before he spoke. "Were those guys weird or were they weird?"

"Both," muttered Julie. "And a little scary, too. But besides that, if Galen did call us here, why didn't he meet us at the stairs?"

"Do you think maybe he's at this Droon Quest thing?" asked Neal.

Eric scanned the forest. "Maybe. At least now we know that this is Bangledorn Forest. It's ruled by a queen named Ortha, I think."

"Right," said Julie. "And Ortha is friends with Keeah. Maybe she can help us find her."

"Finally," Neal added. "After the unfunniest clown and the hugest muscle man in Droon, it'll be good to find some real friends. Let's get moving."

Bangledorn Forest was like a jungle — enormous, dark, and hot. Brightly colored birds began crowing the moment the kids entered.

"Caww! Keee! Rooo-woo!"

Leaves fluttered and hanging vines

twitched above them as they searched for a path.

"It's kind of spooky in here," said Eric.

"Don't worry," said Julie. "This seems pretty much like a rain forest. We studied one in science, remember? We'll be okay. Just stay cool."

"Stay cool?" said Neal, flapping his shirt. "It's a rain forest. It must be a hundred degrees —"

Crack! There was a loud noise in the bushes.

"Run!" said Eric. But they couldn't run.

Something large and swift came crashing through the trees and leaped onto the path in front of them.

Neal jumped. "Holy cow, I mean — *tiger!*"

It was a tiger.

A tiger covered with red fur.

Rowww! It growled loudly, but there was something strange in the sound. At once, the kids knew. This wasn't just any tiger.

"My gosh!" cried Julie. "Could it be? I think it's . . . it's . . . Queen Relna!"

As if it understood Julie's words, the animal slowed. Its red fur rippled from head to tail.

Its black eyes started in fear.

Then the tiger spoke. "My young friends, find Keeah. Tell her the hour has come for me to change, but there is danger. I am being followed. Tell her . . . beware . . . the . . . magic!"

Then, as swiftly as it had appeared, the tiger jumped away through the trees.

"Queen Relna!" Julie yelled. "Wait! Don't go!"

But the red tiger was gone.

Eric stared around into the thick woods. "I don't see anything following her. She sure looked frightened, though."

"You can add me to that list," said Neal. "Man, I wish Keeah were here . . . Whooooa!"

Suddenly, Neal leaped ten feet in the air, twirled once, then shot straight up into a tree.

Julie gaped at him. "How did you do that?"

"I didn't!" Neal cried. "Something *threw* me up here!"

The next thing Eric knew, his feet were yanked out from under him and — "Yikes!" — he, too, was hurled into the tree.

Julie looked at them. "Well, of all the — hey!"

Now she was jerked up from the ground, swung around like a propeller,

and — *fwing!* — thrown into the tree with Neal and Eric.

"Who *did* that?" she howled.

The only answer was a sound — *thumpa! thumpa!* — as heavy footsteps crashed after the tiger and away into the woods.

Three

The Wonder in the Trees

"Can somebody help me down?" said Neal, doubled over a thick branch. "I can't move."

"My foot is stuck," Eric moaned. "Someone has to unstick me. . . ."

"Stop complaining," snapped Julie, trying to get her arms free. "Help me instead!"

"Shhh!" Neal hissed. "Somebody's coming!"

The kids looked down.

Trotting up the path was a spry old man. He wore a ragged cloak with a hood, thick glasses, and a long, droopy mustache.

"Hey, sir!" Julie called out to the man. "Can you help us down from this tree?"

The old man stopped under the tree and blinked up through his glasses at the kids. "Oh, my gosh! It's you!"

Krrripp! The stranger tugged off the mustache, tore off the glasses, and shook off the old clothes.

Julie squealed when she saw who it was. "Keeah! It's Keeah! It's her! It's you!"

It was Princess Keeah.

"I'm so glad you're here!" she said brightly.

Keeah's crown shone in her long blond hair. On her back she carried her mother's magic harp.

"How did you know to come to Droon?" she asked as she quickly climbed the tree and helped her friends down one by one.

"Galen was in the sink at school!" said Eric, rubbing his ankle. "Well, his face was."

"Then the chalk wrote *She is lost* on the board," Neal added. "We figured Galen meant that you were lost."

"Me? Lost?" Keeah said, her eyes widening.

"The last time we saw you, you flew away on a big bird," said Julie. "We were worried. I guess Galen was, too."

"Oh, no," said Keeah. "I've been in disguise searching for my mother. Now everyone thinks I'm lost —"

"Plus, we saw your mom," said Neal. "She said she needs to change shapes, but somebody's following her. She also said, 'Beware the magic.'"

Keeah held up her hand. "Wait." She

closed her eyes for a moment. Then she sighed. "No. She is no longer nearby. Come on. We'd better get to Bangledorn City right away. We need to tell everyone we're safe. This way!"

The princess pushed some leaves aside and jumped onto a narrow path through the trees.

As the kids followed, they told Keeah about Tarok and Slag and the attack in the woods.

Keeah listened carefully. "After I left you, I tracked my mother here to the forest. I went in disguise when I realized someone was hunting for her."

"Can your harp help you find her?" asked Eric. Keeah's magic harp used to belong to her mother. No one knew all the harp's powers, but it had helped the kids many times before.

Keeah held up the small, bow-shaped

instrument and touched a row of colorful gems called story stones. They showed events in Queen Relna's life. One of the stones took the form of a red tiger. The next two stones were missing.

"My harp won't help me here," said Keeah. "No magic is allowed in Bangledorn Forest. Long ago, the forest was proclaimed a place of peace. It's an ancient law of Droon."

Julie frowned. "Sounds like somebody isn't playing by the rules."

"Yeah, the invisible dude," said Neal, rubbing his sore arms. "Met him. Didn't like him."

The princess entered a thick hedge of bushes, then stopped and smiled.

"Even though the laws of Droon do not permit magic here," she said, "amazing things can still happen. If you know where to look."

She pushed through a wall of bright flowering bushes. "Behold . . . Bangledorn City!"

The kids looked around them.

"Holy cow!" said Neal. "It's like the ultimate tree house, except — it's a tree city!"

It was true.

Spreading far up into the distance was a city built of tree houses of all sizes. The houses were made from branches and their roofs were thatched with fat green leaves.

Giant towers were carved into massive tree trunks. They loomed like friendly old men watching over the city. Bridges made of woven vines dangled from one tall tree to the next.

Some of the tallest houses even poked through the very top of the forest.

"This is so amazing!" Eric exclaimed.

"It is one of the great wonders of

Droon," said Keeah, her eyes beaming. "Let's go in."

Boom-thum! Boom-thum! Drums pounded as soon as the children entered the city.

At once, a troop of furry green monkeys scampered down from the trees and surrounded the visitors. "Keeah!" they cried. "Keeah is found!"

Another group of monkeys appeared from nowhere. With them was a tall old man wearing a long blue robe and a tall wizard's hat.

"Galen!" said Keeah, rushing to him.

The wizard hugged the princess as if she were his own daughter. "Ah, my dear Keeah. I searched for you, then lost you in the forest. Even I am not allowed to use my powers here."

He turned to Eric, Neal, and Julie. "Forgive me for not meeting you at the stairs. I

was called to the city. I'm glad you found Keeah so quickly."

Julie laughed. "Well, Keeah sort of found us."

"Yeah, up a tree!" added Neal. "Some kind of invisible dude tossed us up there."

"Invisible?" said Galen with a quick look at Keeah. "So, there is magic here. . . ."

"Keeah! Children!" a happy voice chirped.

It was Max, an eight-legged spider troll with big eyes and orange hair. He scampered down from a tree and hugged Keeah as Galen had.

"You're all here just in time," Max said. "Eric, Julie, Neal, the Droon Quest is today. It happens only once every seven years. It's a great contest of skill and endurance. And also of fun!"

"Cool. Fun is my best sport!" said Neal.

Galen turned to a flight of log stairs ascending to a palace in the trees. "The Quest will begin soon. And for that we must see Ortha, leader of the Bangledorn monkeys. But first, tell me what you have seen. Or, in the case of this invisible person, what you have *not* seen!"

On their way to the palace, Eric, Julie, and Neal told Galen about Tarok and Slag, the invisible attacker, and the red tiger.

"Queen Relna told us, 'Beware the magic,'" Eric added. "We don't know what that means."

Galen paused on the stairs to Ortha's palace. "It means someone is defying the ancient laws of Droon. Upsetting the peace that graces this wonderful forest."

"Who would do that?" asked Julie.

"Only a sorcerer or wizard could," Galen replied. "Since Lord Sparr is in hiding, I can only guess who is behind this unlawful use of magic."

Keeah looked at her friends, then at Galen. "Who *is* behind it?"

Galen's eyes narrowed as he spoke the name. "Witch Demither."

Eric shuddered. They all did.

Galen went on. "As you know, Demither's powers for evil are second only to those of Lord Sparr himself. But what she wants is far from clear. Seven years ago Demither appeared at the last Quest, and she and the queen fought. Oh, a bitter sight it was."

"Who won?" asked Neal. "I'll bet it was the queen."

"No one wins such a conflict," Galen said sharply. "A battle of angry words ending in silence. Demither demanded something. The queen refused. I never learned what it was about. But it was clear to me that the witch held some secret power over Keeah's mother."

"Demither is bad to the core," said Max, snarling. "I do not trust her an inch!"

They stood before the doors of Ortha's palace. Then Galen turned to look out over the forest. The black sea churned angrily in the distance.

"If indeed there is dark magic in the wood today," the wizard said, "then clearly we must be watchful. We must be careful. All of us."

Bong! A deep gonging sound boomed over the trees.

And the great wooden doors of the palace swung open.

Four

Into the Arena

The giant doors parted and out strode Ortha, ruler of the Bangledorn monkeys.

She was tall and slender and her green fur glistened in the sunlight. She wore a long blue cape and a crown made of sharp purple leaves.

She smiled warmly at the kids.

"Welcome, all of you, to our forest," she said. "Keeah, children, I am glad you are safe. You have arrived just in time. The

Quest begins this afternoon. Let me show you . . ."

They entered a giant green room. The leafy ceiling was held aloft by massive wooden pillars.

"This is so cool," Neal said. "It's like being outside . . . inside!"

The sunlight and warm breezy air flowed through the open sides of the palace, fluttering the leaves.

Wood chimes clattered gently from the ceiling.

"It's so magical here," said Julie.

"We Bangledorns live entirely without magic," Ortha said as she swept through the hall. "That is why Queen Relna chose our forest as the site of the Droon Quest. Everyone, no matter who they are, has a chance to win."

Galen turned to Ortha. "Alas, Keeah and the children have seen magic in the woods today. Queen Relna is nearby, but she is not safe. An unknown creature is following her invisibly."

Ortha drew in her breath sharply. "Our forest was never meant to be the battleground of evil forces. But we cannot delay the Quest."

They passed from the room and out onto a balcony overlooking the vast forest.

Below the palace, on the forest floor, was a large open arena. In the center was a field. A great throng of people and strange creatures from every corner of Droon were gathering there. Banners waved, and flags of all sizes and colors flapped over the tents and incoming wagons.

Julie pointed to a long winding path through the forest below. "What's that?" she asked.

"That is the course for the Quest," Ortha said. "Each team races in chariots. The

course twists and turns like a snake and ends at the sea."

"It looks so cool," said Neal. "Can we race?"

The Bangledorn ruler nodded. "Yes, but as with all true quests, it will not be easy. You must race once around the arena, then enter the forest. There you will find obstacles."

"What kind of obstacles?" asked Eric.

"First the walls of fire!" said Max, his eyes growing large. "Then an angry raging river!"

"After that you must race on foot," said Ortha. "Across the beach and across a bridge. "

"A bridge to where?" asked Julie.

"Ah, this is the most wonderful part," said Galen. "On this very day every seven years, an island appears offshore at sundown. When Relna founded the Quest, she chose the island as the place where the Quest would end. It is on the island that the winner will find the prize."

"But you must be quick!" said Max. "The island appears for only a few moments before it vanishes again — for another seven years!"

"Another secret of Droon," Julie said. "Neat!"

"But what is the prize?" asked Eric. "A gold medal? A trophy? Treasure?"

Galen shook his head. "Many legends have grown up about the prize. But it is something worth far more than gold or jewels. For the one meant to win, the prize is what he or she wants most. For all others, it is worthless. The Quest prize is the only magic allowed here."

"Could the prize be a cure for my mother?" Keeah asked breathlessly.

"It could indeed," said Ortha. "Your

mother hoped that someday you would win the prize. It is not only a great honor, but a test of a truly special person."

Keeah looked at the gathering crowd. Then she unslung her harp. "I will try my best." She handed the harp to Galen. "I guess I won't be needing this."

The gong sounded again, and Ortha smiled at the children. "It is time to enter the arena!"

The children, with Max and Keeah leading the way, descended into the Quest arena.

There were all kinds of games and sporting events being held before the big Quest.

One purple Lumpy in a yellow warm-up suit was tossing a large leather ball at a stone wall.

"Okay," said Neal. "The catapult contest."

Nearby a pair of slithery creatures with tiny heads raced into the trees as crowds cheered.

Beyond that, a handful of green monkeys leaped onto vines and swung to see how far they could go before jumping off into a small pond.

Julie grinned. "I love it! It's like the Olympics in our world. I want to be in a race."

"Look!" Max shouted. "The chariots!"

Eric whistled when he saw them. "Oh, cool!"

Before them stood a giant parking lot full of chariots, ready for the Quest.

Each chariot was like a fancy open cart hitched to a single pilka. Some had wings flying up from the back. Others had double sets of wheels. Some had seats, others you stood up in.

But all of them looked very fast.

Keeah hopped into a sleek purple one. "This is the one I'm choosing," she said excitedly. "I love the wings in the back. Besides, it's big enough for four. Would you like to race along with me?"

Julie jumped up and down. "Yes, yes, yes! I'd love to!"

"You bet," said Neal. "Vrrrm-vrrrrrm!"

Eric glanced around at the crowd. "But let's not forget our homework. Galen said to be watchful. If there's magic here, it means someone is disobeying the law."

"I'll watch out for cheaters," said Neal. "But I'm running if I see someone invisible!"

"How can you *see* someone who's invisible?" asked Julie.

Keeah laughed, then stopped suddenly and looked around. "You sense them. . . ."

Eric turned to her. "Are you saying you sense something now?"

Before Keeah could answer, a loud voice yelled behind them. "Out of the way, please!"

A yellow wagon rumbled into the field.

It was Tarok! He seemed to stare at Keeah as he drove his wagon into the arena.

"Tarok the clown is here!" he bellowed. "My show begins in half an hour. You'll laugh so hard . . . you'll cry!"

Julie pulled Keeah close. "That's him!" she whispered as the wagon rolled by. "Tarok is the strange man we told you about."

Keeah watched the yellow wagon rumble away. "It's odd. I feel something, but I'm not sure what —"

"Keeah," said Max, pulling her by the hand. "The vine trials! Everyone's asking for you!"

Keeah took one last look at Tarok's

wagon, then turned and smiled at the kids. "I've always wanted to compete in the high vines event. I'll meet you back here right away. . . ."

"We'll stay here and snoop around," said Eric as Max led Keeah into the crowd.

Julie glanced at Eric and Neal. "What was that all about? Do you think Keeah really sensed something? Maybe magic in the air?"

"It's kind of odd that Tarok should come along just when she felt something," Neal said.

"Maybe not so odd," said Eric, gazing after Tarok. "There's something strange about that clown. I don't trust him, or Slag, either."

"Where is Slag, anyway?" Julie asked.

Neal glanced around the crowd. "You can't miss that guy. Even his muscles have muscles!"

"Both of those dudes give me the major creeps," Julie added.

Eric gave a quick nod. "I'd like to see what else Tarok has in that wagon of his. What do you say we do some serious spying?"

"That gets my vote," said Neal. They all started after Tarok's wagon.

Suddenly, a cry rang out over the arena. "Help! Princess Keeah's in trouble!"

Five

A Princess in Trouble!

The kids rushed through the crowd. Everyone was staring up into the tall trees at the top of the forest.

Keeah stood on a single slim vine that hung between two trees like a high wire.

But something was wrong.

The vine she was on was rippling and quivering under her as if someone were shaking it.

Eric looked over at the far tree. "Someone's pulling on Keeah's vine. She'll fall."

"But . . . there's no one there!" said Julie.

"It must be Mr. Invisible!" Neal added. "Tossing people around wasn't bad enough. Now he's messing with our princess!"

In a flash, the kids jumped into action. They started climbing a rope ladder to the top of the first tree.

"Hang in there, Keeah!" Neal yelled up.

"Faster!" said Eric, keeping his eye on the princess as he climbed. "She won't be able to stay on much longer."

They reached a small wooden platform at the top of the tree. It looked as if the vine Keeah was standing on was being wobbled sharply from the platform on the far tree. She was desperately trying to keep her balance.

"What do we do now?" Julie asked.

Eric looked around. Hanging vines dangled all around them. "We do what they do in circuses all the time."

"Juggle?" asked Neal.

"No, like on the trapeze," said Eric. He grabbed one of the vines and tugged on it. "This should hold me," he said.

"Are you nuts?" said Neal. "You fell off the ropes in gym today!"

Eric gave Neal a look. "I fell off because you fell on me! Besides, do you have another idea? Keeah can't use magic. She's like us now. She needs help." He paused. "From people who know what they're doing."

"Okay, okay, don't rub it in," said Neal. "Julie and I will hold the vine tight to make sure it doesn't break. You go and try to reach her. When you do —"

"We'll haul you both in," said Julie. "Simple teamwork. But please be careful."

Eric tied the end of the vine tightly around his waist. He took a deep breath. "Wish me luck."

"Luck," said Neal. "And hurry!"

Eric hoped he could do it. He wasn't very good with ropes. Not as bad as Neal, but still not very good. Still, he had to try.

As soon as he stepped out, the vine strung between the trees shook some more.

"Ohhh!" the crowd gasped.

Eric's heart was racing a mile a minute. He could hardly breathe. He felt hot and cold at the same time. "If this doesn't work . . ." he whispered to himself.

"Never mind! It will work! It has to!"

Neal and Julie tried to hold the vine steady, but it shook even more violently.

Keeah glanced at Eric, her eyes filled with fear. "Please be careful . . ." she began.

Eric edged farther out, then — *snap!* — the vine broke under them.

Keeah fell.

Eric leaped for her, his arms outstretched. "Grab on to me!" he cried.

On his way down, their hands met. Eric clutched Keeah's wrists, his vine pulled tight, and they swung back to the tree. Keeah grabbed the rope ladder and held it tight.

"Eric — thank you!" she gasped.

Eric's heart was still racing. "Never mind that. We need to catch whoever did this!"

Together they jumped to the ground. Julie and Neal scrambled down after them. They ran to the far tree. But they saw no one. Whoever had been shaking the vine was nowhere in sight.

Suddenly — *thumpa! thumpa!* The

ground thudded and leaves fluttered in the forest.

"It's Mr. Invisible!" said Neal. "After him!"

The kids tore through the bushes. The leaves crashed this way and that. They nearly caught up to the invisible creature, but lost the trail when it hooked out of the forest into the arena.

"There must be a thousand people here," said Julie as they pushed into the bustling crowd.

"Keep looking for clues," said Eric.

"I'm looking," whispered Neal. "But so far, I haven't spotted anything —"

"Wait!" said Keeah. "Look there, footprints!"

As they watched, large footprints appeared one after another on the ground nearby. The prints wove carefully through the crowd and led to a wagon.

A yellow wagon.

Tarok's wagon.

"Aha!" Julie said with a gasp. "I knew Tarok was a part of this."

"But what is Tarok up to?" Keeah asked. "And why is he doing what he's doing?"

All of a sudden — *honka-honka!* — a noise rose up out over the crowd.

"Come one! Come all!" a familiar voice bellowed. "See Droon's funny man! I am Tarok the clown! My act is so funny, you'll just *die* laughing!"

Six

Droon's Funniest Man?

Honka! Honka!

The crowd cheered as Tarok ran around honking his horn on a small stage near the wagon.

"Welcome, one and all!" the little man called out. Then he pointed directly at Keeah. "I see we have Queen Relna's daughter here! And what rhymes with daughter? How about . . . water!"

Tarok then picked up a bucket with the

word *water* written on the side, rushed at the audience, and emptied it over them.

Everyone screamed and ducked.

But it wasn't water, it was glitter. It showered gently over the crowd.

"Now watch this!" said Tarok as he began to juggle three glass balls while standing on one foot. "Isn't this amazing?"

"I wish I could juggle," Neal whispered.

Julie gave him a look as the kids crept forward. "Neal, we think he's the bad guy."

Neal shrugged. "But juggling is so cool."

Tarok caught the balls and stuffed them in a pocket. "And now for something mystical and mysterious!" he boomed.

He raised his hands and — *poof!*

A cloud of red smoke exploded on the stage.

When the smoke cleared, Slag was standing there. All seven feet of him. The crowd cheered.

"Mr. Invisible, live and in person!" Neal said.

Eric snorted. "Mystical and mysterious, huh? It looks like magic to me."

Keeah frowned. "So it was Slag who tried to knock me off the vine? And it was him chasing my mother?"

Tarok waved his hands at the crowd. "I am pleased to present Slag, the mightiest man in Droon. Slag, show them — especially the little ones — just how strong you are. . . ."

Slag squinted out over the crowd, then fixed his eyes on the kids. As he did, he began to bend a long iron bar. He groaned, he growled, he snarled, he grunted. When he was done, the bar was twisted into a giant knot.

Neal nudged Eric. "Do you get the feeling he wants to do that to us?"

"He's trying to scare us," said Keeah.

"Because we suspect them of . . . of . . . oh, my gosh! She's here. . . . My mother is here!"

Eric whirled on his heels. "Where? Do you see her?"

"No," Keeah whispered, closing her eyes. "She's . . . trapped. She's hurt. I feel it. . . ."

Julie slapped her forehead. "Of course!"

"Of course what?" said Neal.

"It all makes sense now," Julie whispered. "That big net Slag had. Tarok saying they were going fishing. This weird wagon of theirs. Mr. Invisible. Don't you see?"

"Yes!" said Neal. Then he shook his head. "Well, not really."

Julie pulled the kids close. "Tarok and Slag are the ones who trapped Queen Relna! Not only that, they have her in their wagon!"

Keeah's eyes grew wide. "I'm going in there."

Eric saw blue sparks shoot suddenly from the tips of Keeah's fingers. "We're all going in," he said. "Together."

"Yeah, we'll bust them good," Neal added.

They started edging away from the crowd.

"Stop!" Tarok snapped, pointing a sharp finger at the kids. "Don't go. The fun is just beginning. I need a volunteer. You there with the silly grin. I need you!"

The crowd turned to Neal.

"Who, me?" Neal pointed to himself. "No, sorry. I don't volunteer. It always gets me in trouble. Like the time I cleaned the erasers for Mrs. Michaels and got chalk dust all over her clothes? I nearly got detention. Or the time I —"

Eric pulled him close. "Neal, this is the perfect plan! Tarok will probably just pretend to pull eggs from your ear or something."

"I don't want eggs in my ear!" Neal cried.

"But you can keep an eye on Tarok and Slag, while we snoop inside their mystery wagon," Julie pleaded. "It's the only way."

"Maybe he'll teach you to juggle," whispered Eric.

"Really? Juggle?" Neal blinked. "Okay." He jumped onto the stage.

"Right this way," Tarok said as Neal stumbled up next to him. "We'll do a bit of simple illusion. Simple and fun."

"It's magic, make no mistake," Keeah whispered to her friends. "Come on."

As they began to circle around the crowd, Tarok brought out the three glass balls again.

"Cool," Neal mumbled. He seemed entranced when Tarok started to juggle them once more.

"Keep your eye on the balls," said Tarok. "And one . . . and two . . . and —"

POOF! A great puff of red smoke exploded on the stage. And the three of them were gone.

Tarok, Slag, and Neal.

Gone in a puff of smoke!

Julie gasped. "Where's Neal? Wait a second. I don't like this after all."

Eric watched the smoke rise then begin to fall over the amazed crowd. He didn't like it, either. "Keeah," he said, "is Neal okay? Keeah?"

But the princess had already crept around to the back of Tarok's wagon.

The door creaked once, and she was inside.

Seven

Tarok's Mystery Wagon

When Eric and Julie pulled open the wagon door, they found the inside room empty.

Julie frowned. "Where did Keeah go?"

There was a small door on the opposite wall.

"Did she go back out?" asked Eric. "Oh, man. First Neal, now Keeah. We keep losing people. Let's stick close."

Julie nodded. She crossed to the small

door and pulled it open slowly. As she did, the air seemed to hum and sparkle.

"Holy cow!" she exclaimed.

Eric peeked over her shoulder. He gulped.

The door didn't lead back outside.

It led . . . to another room. And what a room!

It was at least twice the size of their school classroom. And the ceiling was three times as high as the wagon itself!

"No wonder they could fit a pilka in here," Julie whispered when they stepped in. "They could fit a whole herd of them!"

But it sure didn't look like a stable.

The place was magnificently decorated, as if it were a room in the richest palace. Candles on the walls lit an area of couches, tables, and chairs sitting on a fancy carpet.

Piled along the walls were big traveling chests. They overflowed with gold and

jewels and leather bags filled with glittering coins.

Eric shook his head slowly. "Okay, this is plain crazy. How can you have a wagon that's bigger on the inside than the outside?"

"Keeah was right," said Julie. "This is no simple illusion. This is magic. Look, there's another door at the far end. Keeah? Keeah!"

Julie ran for the door, but Eric's eye was caught by one chest with jewels tumbling out.

He leaned over. Among the jewels in the chest was a shiny black gem. It was flat and perfectly round.

He picked it up. It glimmered in the candlelight. Then it flickered suddenly in his hand.

"Check this out!" he said. "It looks like

a story stone from Keeah's harp. Julie?" He glanced up.

Julie was staring through the far door. "Eric," she whispered. "Get over here. Now!"

He pushed the stone into his pocket and went to her. He stared past her through the doorway.

"Okay, well, um, this is different," he said.

"Different?" said Julie. "It's weirder than weird."

They were standing at the top of a set of steps that curved down a long way into darkness. The steps seemed to go far below the ground that the wagon was sitting on.

"I guess we have to go down?" Julie asked.

"I guess we do," said Eric.

Quietly, the two friends tramped down the steps. The stairs were covered with a kind of thick slime. They kept curving downward.

"I wish Neal were here —" said Julie.

"Me, too."

"— so he could go first!" Julie finished.

Eric tried to laugh. He couldn't. He was scared.

What had happened to Neal? And where were they going? And who *were* Tarok and Slag, anyway?

Finally, the steps ended. Eric and Julie came out into a stone chamber. The floor was wet. And it smelled like the beach.

Like seawater.

It was much darker and colder than the other rooms. But Eric breathed a sigh of relief.

Keeah was there.

And she was not alone.

"Mother . . . Mother . . ." she murmured.

Keeah was standing next to a cage. The red tiger lay inside, almost still, breathing very slowly.

"I feel so helpless!" she said. "Look at her. She's sick. She can hardly breathe."

"Maybe it's because she needs to change into another shape," said Eric. "And she can't because of the cage."

"She needs to be set free," said Julie.

Keeah reached her hand toward the cage.

Kkkkk! A bolt of red light shot out from the bars and struck Keeah's hand. She snatched it back. "This is a sorcerer's magic! Red light is always a sign of dark magic."

"You should know. . . ." said a cold voice.

Tarok strode from the shadows. Gone

was his clown's nose. His wild blue hair. His silly horn.

He tossed up a glass ball and caught it. "So you've found our little secret. Quite a catch, isn't she? The Queen of Droon. In my little wagon."

"Let her go!" demanded Keeah.

"Mmm . . . no," Tarok replied.

"You know," snarled Eric, "for a funny man, you're not very funny."

Tarok's face twisted into a dark scowl. "No, the fun is over. Now the games begin. Want to play catch?"

Tarok held the ball up in front of Eric.

That's when the kids noticed a tiny shape inside the ball. A shape they all knew.

It was waving at them.

"Oh, my gosh," said Eric. "It's Neal!"

Julie gasped. "You let him out of there! Right now!"

"No," said Tarok, backing away. "Slag, come forward!"

The giant stepped out of the shadows behind Tarok. He held his pretzel-shaped iron bar.

"I bend you like a bar," Slag grunted.

Eric glanced at Keeah and Julie. "I was right. This is definitely *not* funny!"

Eight

The Quest Begins!

Tarok stepped over to the cage and waved his hand over it.

Kkkkk! In a violent burst of light, the cage was empty, and Tarok was holding a second ball.

In the ball was the red tiger.

"How did you do that?" demanded Keeah. "Where did you get that power?"

"Yeah!" Eric growled. "Just who *are* you?"

Tarok stepped back toward the shadows. "We're just two fellows with a job to finish. . . ."

"That's right," said Slag. "She'd be mad at us if we failed."

"She?" said Julie. "She who?"

Keeah's eyes widened. She began to tremble.

"Witch Demither!" she hissed. "She's where they get their power!"

"How very clever of you, Princess," Tarok said, bowing slightly. "We do odd jobs for the witch, it's true. We're her *legs*, I guess you could say. Demither told us to catch the tiger, so . . ."

"I caught her," grunted Slag. "Me and my net. In the woods."

"Of course!" said Eric. "You came straight out of the water. That's where Demither rules. And this magic wagon . . . it even smells like fish!"

"Ha!" Tarok laughed. "Using Demither's magic, we'll have more than fish. We'll win the Quest and the prize, a fabulous treasure of gold and jewels! It's our reward for catching the queen."

"You're evil!" Julie cried. "You're not allowed to use magic here. Especially witch magic!"

Then — *bong!* — Ortha's gong sounded outside, signaling that the Quest was about to begin.

"I'd love to stay and chat," Tarok said, "but Demither wants the queen and we want that prize! Oh, I almost forgot . . . catch —"

Taking the ball with Neal inside, he tossed it up to the high ceiling.

"Don't break Neal!" cried Julie. She jumped for the ball. But somewhere near the ceiling it burst. Neal popped out — full size — and collapsed to the floor.

Tarok and Slag leaped away into the shadows.

"They're escaping!" said Keeah. "After them!"

Suddenly, the walls around the kids began to collapse. *Flonk! Clang!* The room got smaller.

"Let's get out before it traps us!" cried Eric.

He helped Neal up and they all jumped after Tarok but — *splat!* — they found themselves facedown in the mud outside the wagon.

Flap! Blonk! Plink! The wagon kept changing.

"It's becoming . . . a chariot!" cried Julie.

The great gong sounded once more.

"The Quest is starting!" yelled Neal.

Tarok laughed icily. He snapped the reins hard and his pilka charged into the arena.

Keeah's fingers sparked. "I'll stop them!"

"No, Keeah, don't do it," said Eric, rushing to her. "We'll stop them the regular way."

"Yeah," said Neal, running over to her chariot. "We'll chase them!"

Keeah stared at the chariot, then at her friends. Then she gave them a smile. "Let's go!"

The kids hopped into the chariot. Galen's pilka, Leep, was already hitched up to it. Keeah snapped the reins and the chariot thundered onto the race course.

Whoosh! A cloud of dust blossomed up from the starting line as a dozen other chariots raced around the arena.

But Tarok and Slag were far in the lead. Their chariot charged ahead, rounded the arena, and shot into the forest.

Already the sun was falling behind the trees.

"We have to catch him soon," Julie said, "or we'll be too late. The island will be gone."

"Faster, Leep!" Keeah said, and the pilka jumped ahead with a burst of speed.

Eric gripped the sides of the chariot tighter. "It's okay to go fast, but please drive safely!"

Leaves and vines flapped and whizzed by as they drove deeper into the forest. Right, left, right. The course twisted and turned sharply.

The path grew narrow. Then something loomed ahead of them.

It was the first of the obstacles.

"Uh-oh. Flame walls ahead!" Neal called out. "Prepare to be charcoal broiled!"

A wall of orange flame rose up on each

side of the narrowing path. The fire lashed out like fingers trying to claw whatever passed through.

But Tarok didn't slow down.

He shot a handful of silver dust into the path, and — *k-k-k-zing!* — the flames froze instantly.

"Thank you for your magic, Demither!" he said as he drove his chariot swiftly between the frozen flames.

As soon as he passed through, the fire crackled angrily to life again.

Hrrr! Leep reared up, nearly tipping the chariot over. She wouldn't go on. She stamped her feet on the ground and began backing up.

"She won't ride into the flames!" Keeah said.

Julie looked around. "I have an idea. I saw it in a movie once. Wish me luck —"

"Luck!" said Eric.

Julie pulled two leaves from a nearby bush, jumped up onto Leep's back, and slapped the leaves over the pilka's head so it couldn't see sideways.

"Try it now!" Julie called back.

Keeah urged Leep to move forward.

Hrrr! Leep whinnied loudly, then raced between the fiery walls and out the other side.

"Yes!" Julie whipped the leaves off.

Eric helped her back into the chariot and slapped her a high five. "Nice work, Julie!"

"The next one's up to you guys," she said.

Keeah drove the chariot hard over the path.

Eric looked ahead even as he clutched the sides of the chariot more tightly.

He knew — they all knew — that they needed to do more than stop Tarok and Slag. They had to win the prize. Eric remembered Galen's words. For the one meant to win, the prize was what he or she wanted most.

Eric knew what Keeah wanted. It's what they all wanted. A cure for Queen Relna.

But it sure wasn't going to be easy!

Clank! Plonk! Slag began tossing iron bars out the back of their speeding chariot. The bars struck the path and bounced up at the kids.

Keeah tried to drive the chariot around the bars, but one of them hit a wheel. The chariot bounced. So did Eric and Neal. They shot out of the chariot like cannonballs from a cannon.

"Whoooa!" cried Eric as they went

hurtling toward a tree. "We're gonna get smushed!"

Suddenly — *fwing!* — a thick net of vines flashed down from above. Eric tumbled into the net unhurt. Neal shot in next to him. They looked up. A handful of green Bangledorn monkeys waved from the high trees. "Yee-yee!"

"Thanks!" Eric yelled up.

"It's nice to have friends in high places!" Neal added.

Eric and Neal leaped down from the net just as their chariot passed underneath. *Plop! Plop!* They dropped down right next to Julie and Keeah.

"Glad to have you back!" said Keeah, laughing.

Then another laugh broke through the forest.

"This will stop you!" Tarok yelled back as he sped into the next turn in the course.

"What will stop us?" asked Julie.

Then they heard it.

Sploosh! Crash! Splash!

"Oh, no!" cried Keeah. "The raging river!"

Nine

Island of Magic

A wild river crashed and surged across the course, sending cold white spray high in the air.

Tarok slowed his wagon only long enough to shoot more sparkly dust across the water.

K-k-k-zing! The river turned as smooth as glass. It froze into a flat road of ice.

"Aha!" Slag cheered, snapping hard on

* 86 *

the reins and driving their pilka across the ice.

"Hurry," said Julie. "Maybe we can get across before he changes it back —"

Too late. *Splursh!* The river exploded again into whitecapped rapids the instant Tarok and Slag reached the far side.

Keeah pulled Leep to a stop on the near bank and jumped out of the chariot. "We can't fail at this. We need to get the prize. We need to!"

"We won't fail," said Julie. "We'll just have to get across the old-fashioned way."

Neal stepped back from the churning river bank. "You want us to swim across *that?*"

Julie smiled. "Not if we can help it!" She pointed up. Above their heads were dozens of long, thick vines hanging down from the tall trees.

"We swing across to the far side," she said.

"Oh, man," sighed Neal. "It's like I never left gym class." Then he shrugged. "But, hey, you gotta do what you gotta do."

They each grabbed a long vine, ran back, and leaped from the ground.

Fwit! Fwit! Fwit! Fwit! The four friends soared over the river's crashing waves.

Plop! Plop! Plop! Plop! They landed safely on the far bank. They picked themselves up and plowed through one last row of trees.

Beyond them lay a strip of white sandy beach.

On the beach, jutting out into the water, was a narrow footbridge.

And Tarok's chariot was racing toward it.

"We'll have to go the rest of the way on foot," said Keeah. "Come on. Let's run like the wind."

The four friends raced across the sand as fast as they could. At first, the black sea seemed peaceful and almost golden in the fading light.

But as they drew nearer, the water rumbled and the ground quaked. The sea churned wildly, spitting up large, white-capped waves.

"The island," Keeah said. "It's coming!"

Ka-fooom! The sea broke open and a rocky point of land came thrusting up from the black depths. It was as if a small mountain were being pushed out of the earth, through the water, and into the light of day.

Waves bubbled and hissed and swirled all around the land, then went calm.

In the center of the island was a perfectly white stone. On the stone lay a wooden bowl.

It was plain and battered.

It was not encrusted with jewels or gold.

It had no markings on it.

It was just a bowl.

But the instant the fading sunlight struck it, the air around it turned a hundred colors.

The bowl itself glowed and sparkled.

And so did the water in the bowl.

"Oh, my gosh," said Keeah, racing to the bridge. "That's the prize. . . ."

Eric could tell — they could all tell — it wasn't just seawater rippling in a simple wooden bowl.

It was what the true winner wanted most.

"Keeah, the prize is for you," said Eric.

"If Tarok were meant to win, it would be a pile of treasure. But it's not. It must be . . . the cure."

"Run," said the princess. "Run! RUN!"

They raced across the footbridge as fast as their legs could carry them.

But it wasn't fast enough.

Tarok and Slag reached the end of the bridge and leaped onto the island.

"The prize!" Tarok howled, raising his arms in victory. "The prize is mine!"

Ten

A Spell from the Past

Tarok grabbed the bowl from the stone. He stared at it.

"What's this?" he snarled. "This is the legendary prize? It's nothing but an old wooden bowl!"

"Where is the treasure?" Slag boomed. He stuck his nose in the bowl and took a sniff. "This smells like nothing! I want a real prize!"

Before the kids could get to the island,

Tarok and Slag began fighting over the bowl.

"Give it to me!" said Tarok.

"No, it's mine!" Slag boomed.

Suddenly, the bowl slipped through their fingers. It hung in the air for a moment.

Then it crashed to the ground.

Sploosh! The golden liquid splashed out, drained through the rocks, and was washed into the black sea.

"No!" Keeah gasped, jumping onto the island. "That was the prize. It was magic!"

"Magic⸮" said Tarok. He looked at Keeah, then at the bowl, then at Slag. "You numbskull!"

"Me⸮" grunted Slag. "You did it!"

The two men began to slap each other.

Keeah's fingertips shot off blue sparks. "Give me the glass ball now! My mother must change her shape or she'll die!"

Neal and Julie grabbed Tarok by the arms.

"Okay, okay!" the little man said. He tugged the glass ball from a pocket, tossed it up, and — *k-k-k-zing!* — the ball sizzled and sparked, then burst away to nothing in a puff of red smoke.

The tiger appeared before them, lying on the ground, its head resting on its giant paws.

Keeah knelt next to her.

The queen gave out a long, quivering breath. "Keeah, without the cure, only Demither has the power to alter this spell. No one else may do it."

But the princess's eyes flashed with determination. "No. There must be another way. It can't end like this!"

At that moment, Eric's pocket felt hot as if something in it were burning.

"Whoa," he said. "I totally forgot."

He dug his hand in his pocket and pulled out the black gemstone. "I found this in Tarok's wagon," he said. "It's just the right shape to be a story stone from your harp. I thought it might be one of the missing ones."

Keeah held the gem in her hand. "It *is* one of the stones," she said. "I know it is —"

The moment she touched it, the black gem began to flicker in Keeah's hand. And as it did, a halo of bright red light began to swirl around her.

Then the light covered her mother.

The tiger howled a sudden, unearthly sound.

Slag stepped back. "Red light! She has . . . witch power!"

Tarok gaped at Keeah. "But I thought only Demither could do that. The princess . . . she has Demither's power!"

Julie frowned. "For your information, Keeah is a very good wizard —"

Eric turned to Tarok and stared at him fiercely. "Where did you find this stone? Tell me!"

Tarok shriveled under Eric's gaze. "Years ago in the Panjibarrh Hills! I saw Demither and the princess alone together —"

"That's impossible!" Julie snapped. "She would never be alone with that horrible witch!"

"I saw them together," Tarok went on. "Demither held the princess's hands. Strange light flowed between them. Red light. Just like right now! That's where I found the black gem. Now — let — me — go!"

With a burst of strength, Tarok wriggled free of Julie and Neal and — *poof!* — the air filled with smoke. In the confusion, Tarok leaped to the bridge, and Slag with him. Together, they raced to the shore.

But the kids couldn't tear their eyes away from the queen. She had already begun to change.

The tail was first. Then the legs. And the back.

They all turned silvery and black.

"Keeah," the queen purred, "you have saved me. I don't know how you have the power . . . but you do have it." The queen struggled to her feet and crawled to the shore.

"Mother, is it true what Tarok said?" Keeah asked. "About the witch . . . and me?"

Relna shuddered as the last of her red fur vanished and the shiny, dark skin spread completely over her.

"That is a secret I will find the answer to," she said. "Now I must go. My next life is the darkest yet. But there will be joy on the other side. Until then, be careful . . . be well . . . I love you!"

With those words, the queen slid beneath the churning waves. The water crashed once, then was still for a long time.

"Oh, Mother . . ." Keeah whispered.

Suddenly — *splash!* — the waves broke open and something soared out.

"Queen Relna!" Julie shouted.

But this time, nothing of the tiger was left. Instead, she was a sleek and slender sea creature.

A dolphin!

As black as ink, the dolphin flew joyously over the waves. She twirled in midair, then slid beneath the sea again. Over and over she soared and dived.

Softly, Keeah said, "She's beautiful!"

"She has always been beautiful," answered a friendly voice above them.

The kids looked up to see Galen standing calmly on the edge of the bridge.

"Come now," he said. "The Quest is over. The staircase has appeared. And already the magical island begins to sink."

The kids climbed onto the bridge.

Splursh! Black waves washed over the new island, and it descended, rumbling and shaking, beneath the sea once more.

In a moment, it was gone.

On shore, Tarok and Slag climbed into their chariot. *Flonk! Blink!* — in seconds, it was a boat again. It motored quickly into the water.

"The bad guys are getting away!" cried Neal.

Galen smiled. "I think Demither has plans for them. They failed today. She won't like that!"

As soon as the boat hit the water,

waves began to toss it about, driving it far out to sea.

"Serves them right," said Julie.

The kids and Galen crossed the bridge back onto the beach, where the magical staircase stood shimmering on the rocky shore.

From the edge of the forest came a familiar shout. "Yee! Yee!"

Ortha stood with a small band of green monkeys, waving to Eric, Julie, and Neal as they raced to the stairs. The kids waved back.

At the bottom of the staircase, Galen handed the princess her harp. "Although it may not seem so, Keeah, today you have won the Quest."

She smiled and hugged Eric, Julie, and Neal. "I couldn't have done it without my friends."

Galen nodded slowly. "Truly, friends like these are also a prize."

Then Keeah set the black story stone in its place on the harp. As she did, the stone flashed for an instant. Then deep within it, as if etched into the gem from inside, was a shape.

A leaping dolphin.

"Only one stone remains to be found," said the wizard. "Only one more change, then the queen of Droon shall take her throne again."

He motioned to the stairs. "Now, quickly, children, up you go. The Upper World calls you!"

Neal laughed as he jumped onto the staircase. "What a cool Quest," he said. "I can't wait to climb ropes in gym tomorrow. Thanks to Droon, I'm pretty sure I can do anything!"

The three kids headed up the stairs for home.

"Until next time," Keeah called to them, her eyes beaming brightly. Then she and Galen turned to watch the dolphin dive and leap across the waves, all the way to the distant horizon.

"I like happy endings," said Julie, racing up to Eric's basement.

Eric flicked on the closet light.

Whoosh! The stairs disappeared beneath them.

"And happy beginnings," Neal added.

Eric grinned. "The in-between stuff is pretty cool, too. Especially when it happens in Droon!"

ABOUT THE AUTHOR

Tony Abbott is the author of more than three dozen funny novels for young readers, including the popular *Danger Guys* books and *The Weird Zone* series. Since childhood he has been drawn to stories that challenge the imagination, and, like Eric, Julie, and Neal, he often dreamed of finding doors that open to other worlds. Now that he is older — though not quite as old as Galen Longbeard — he believes he may have found some of those doors. They are called books. Tony Abbott was born in Ohio and now lives with his wife and two daughters in Connecticut.